Judah Maccabee
Goes to the Doctor

by Ann D. Koffsky

Illustrated by Talitha Shipman

Springfield, NJ • Jerusalem

For Isaac, the newest Koffsky!
And, for the children at the Hebrew Academy of Nassau County, who are brave and get their shots.
-AK

For Michael, who's been there for every doctor's appointment.
-TS

Editorial Consultant: Dr. Robert Koppel, Northwell Hospital

The *mem* (מ), *kaf* (כ), *bet* (ב), and *yud* (י) on Judah's shield spell the word "Maccabee" in Hebrew.

Apples & Honey Press | An imprint of Behrman House and Gefen Publishing House
Behrman House, 11 Edison Place, Springfield, New Jersey 07081
Gefen Publishing House Ltd., 6 Hatzvi Street, Jerusalem 94386, Israel
www.applesandhoneypress.com

Text copyright © 2017 by Ann D. Koffsky
Illustrations copyright © 2017 by Talitha Shipman

ISBN 978-1-68115-522-7

Library of Congress Cataloging-in-Publication Data
Names: Koffsky, Ann D. | Shipman, Talitha, illustrator.
Title: Judah Maccabee goes to the doctor: a story for Hanukkah / by Ann D. Koffsky; illustrated by Talitha Shipman.
Description: Springfield, New Jersey: Apples & Honey Press, [2017] | Summary: As Hanukkah approaches, a caring older
brother discovers that it is not an outward show of strength that wins the trust of his little sister, but inner strength as
he bravely agrees to have the vaccination that will protect them both from threatening illnesses.
Identifiers: LCCN 2016049180 | ISBN 9781681155227
Subjects: | CYAC: Brothers and sisters--Fiction. | Vaccination--Fiction. | Jews--United States--Fiction. | Hanukkah--Fiction.
Classification: LCC PZ7.K81935 Ju 2017 | DDC [E]--dc23 LC record available at https://lccn.loc.gov/2016049180

Design by Virtual Paintbrush | Edited by Amanda Cohen
Printed in China

1 3 5 7 9 8 6 4 2

Judah wanted to be the BEST big
brother ever. Hannah was his only
sister, after all.

But sometimes, it was SOOO hard . . .

Just yesterday, he had built Hannah
the most stupendous tower ever.

But Hannah didn't think it
was all that stupendous.

And this morning he tried to feed her some delicious Choco-monster-delight cereal.

But Hannah didn't seem to think
it was all that delicious, either.

I don't get it, thought Judah, sitting in his blanket fort. *Why doesn't she like the things I do for her?*

FORT JUDAH

"Don't give up, sweetie,"
said his mom.

The first day of Hanukkah was just around the corner.

"Sometimes little sisters can be like that," explained his bubbe, as she and Judah polished the menorah together. "I know how hard you are trying."

dded
nd."

POLISH

"You know," Bubbe continued, "there was another Judah who lived a very long time ago. His name was Judah Maccabee, and he had four brothers."
"Wow! I just have Hannah," said Judah.

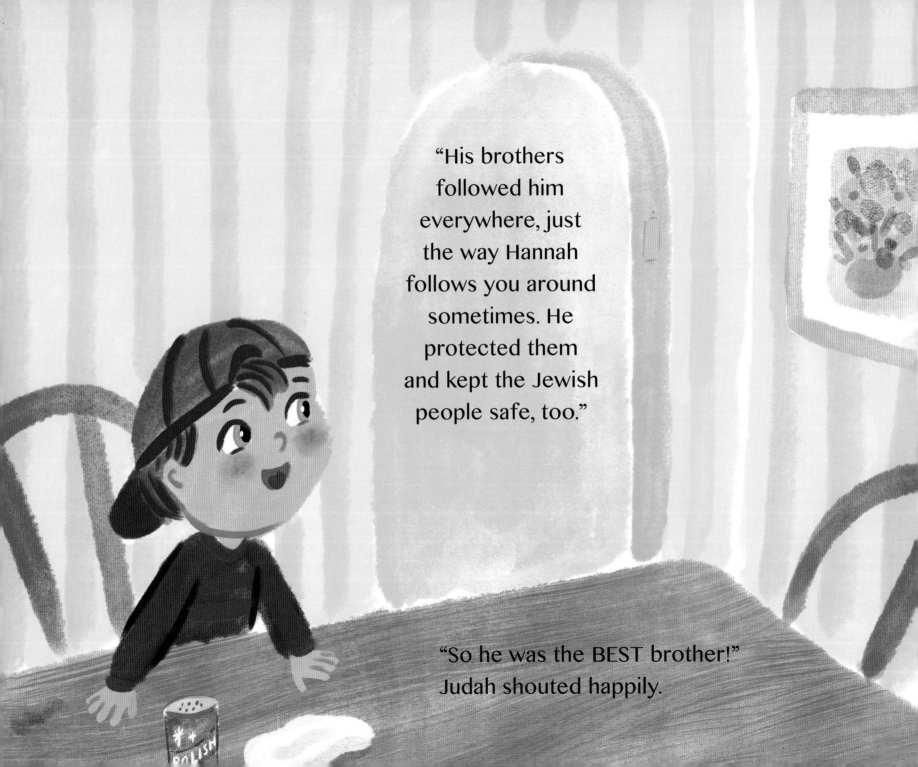

"His brothers followed him everywhere, just the way Hannah follows you around sometimes. He protected them and kept the Jewish people safe, too."

"So he was the BEST brother!" Judah shouted happily.

"One of the best and bravest,"
Bubbe agreed, smiling.

At candle lighting, Bubbe gave Judah a Maccabee shield, just like the one that the first Judah used long ago, when the story of Hanukkah took place.

Judah loved his shield.

It was bright and shiny, with big Hebrew letters on the front. He carried it everywhere ... protecting Hannah whenever he could—from things that were too hot and things that were too cold.

Nothing bad could get past Judah Maccabee's shield!

On the last day of Hanukkah, Dad took Hannah and Judah to the doctor for their yearly check-ups.

It was Hannah's turn first.

Judah watched carefully, holding his shield at the ready!

But Hannah just giggled at the doctor's silly toy and gurgled when the cold stethoscope touched her skin.

Judah smiled happily when the doctor said, "She's a healthy girl!"
"That's because I protect her," he said proudly.
"Keep it up, it's working," said the doctor with a wink.

Then it was Judah's turn.
The doctor checked his ears.

"Helloooo? Anyone in there?"
she called, making Judah laugh.

Then she looked down his throat . . .

. . . and shone a light in his eyes.

"A healthy boy!" The doctor
smiled, and Judah smiled back.
But then the doctor said,
"And now for your shot!"

Judah's smile
quickly went poof!

"Nu-uh, no-way, no-how!" Judah announced, and he quickly hid his arms behind his shield. "Maccabees do NOT get shots!"

"But Judah, a shot is just like a shield," his dad explained. "It protects us from sickness."

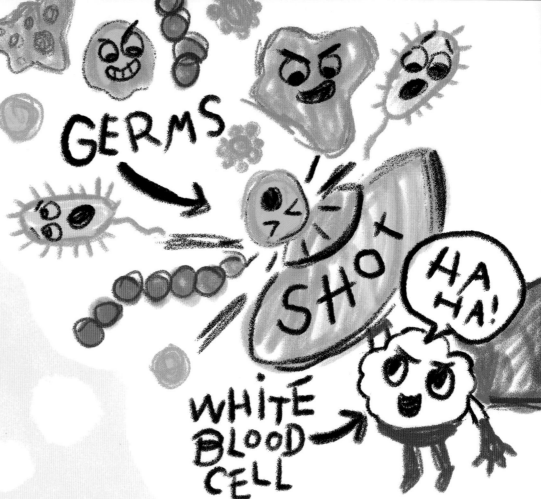

"But I'm not sick, so I don't need a shot."

"Hmm, we may have a problem then!" said his dad.

"Why?" asked Judah.

"You see, Hannah's too young for a shot. But if you get the shot, you'll be protected. You won't be able to get a new sickness, and so she won't be able to catch it from you—keeping you both healthy!"

Hannah looked at Judah
with her big blue eyes.

And that's when Judah understood. Being the BEST and
the bravest wasn't only an outside, shiny-shield thing. It was an
on-the-inside thing too. And that's what he had to show Hannah.

So, Judah Maccabee, bravest warrior of them all, squeezed his eyes shut tight, took a deep breath, and said, "OK!" He stuck out his non-shield arm. "Give it to me! I'm ready."

"Brave boy!" said the doctor and quickly gave Judah his shot.

Ouch! It stung.
Judah cried a
little bit. (Even
Maccabees don't
like shots.)
But then the
ouch went away,
and Judah felt
just fine.

Better than fine.
He'd helped
protect Hannah!

"Judah, you are the best,
BRAVEST brother ever!"
said Dad and the doctor,
together.

And he was.

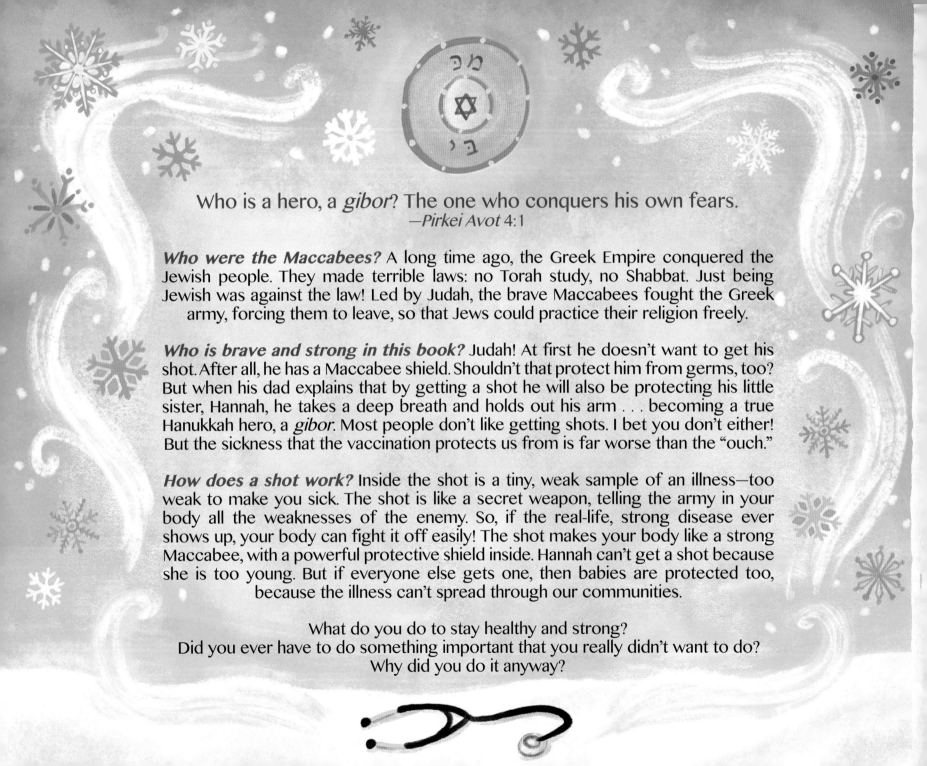

Who is a hero, a *gibor*? The one who conquers his own fears.
—*Pirkei Avot* 4:1

Who were the Maccabees? A long time ago, the Greek Empire conquered the Jewish people. They made terrible laws: no Torah study, no Shabbat. Just being Jewish was against the law! Led by Judah, the brave Maccabees fought the Greek army, forcing them to leave, so that Jews could practice their religion freely.

Who is brave and strong in this book? Judah! At first he doesn't want to get his shot. After all, he has a Maccabee shield. Shouldn't that protect him from germs, too? But when his dad explains that by getting a shot he will also be protecting his little sister, Hannah, he takes a deep breath and holds out his arm . . . becoming a true Hanukkah hero, a *gibor*. Most people don't like getting shots. I bet you don't either! But the sickness that the vaccination protects us from is far worse than the "ouch."

How does a shot work? Inside the shot is a tiny, weak sample of an illness—too weak to make you sick. The shot is like a secret weapon, telling the army in your body all the weaknesses of the enemy. So, if the real-life, strong disease ever shows up, your body can fight it off easily! The shot makes your body like a strong Maccabee, with a powerful protective shield inside. Hannah can't get a shot because she is too young. But if everyone else gets one, then babies are protected too, because the illness can't spread through our communities.

What do you do to stay healthy and strong?
Did you ever have to do something important that you really didn't want to do?
Why did you do it anyway?